THE MOMMY EXCHANGE

Amy Hest · Illustrated by DyAnne DiSalvo-Ryan

Four Winds Press   New York

For Sam and Kate,
who probably wouldn't mind
a mommy exchange
from time to time
—A. H.

For Joey, Vicki, and Tracy
—D. D.-R.

Printed and bound by South China Printing Company, Hong Kong. First American Edition 10 9 8 7 6 5 4 3 2 1

The text of this book is set in 13 point Palmer. The illustrations are rendered in colored pencil and watercolor on
Fabriano paper and reproduced in full color.
Library of Congress Cataloging-in-Publication Data   Hest, Amy. The mommy exchange.
Summary: After concluding that each other's home life is more appealing than their own, two young friends
decide to swap homes and mothers. [1. Mothers—Fiction] I. DiSalvo-Ryan, DyAnne, ill. II. Title. PZ7.H4375Mo
1988 [E] 87-7539 ISBN 0-02-743650-0

In Jason's house they get spaghetti at least twice a week. Not at my house. At my house there's spaghetti only once a week. In the old days my mother got the good kind. It came in a bright red box that said SPAGHETTI PLAIN—ONE POUND.

Now she buys this fancy stuff. The twins, she says, have an easier time with green curls of pasta than with the long, stringy white kind that *I* like. And, my mother always forgets the parmesan.

At Jason's house they get spaghetti with meat sauce or plain, in bowls with funny pictures on the bottom and sometimes on paper plates left over from a birthday party. And Jason's mother never forgets the parmesan.

Whenever I go to Jason's, we get to ride motorcycles in the hallway and around the living room and through the dining room, if we're careful. In his house we're allowed to use sirens with batteries.

My mother says sirens wake up babies. And there are no motorcycles in her living room, because, she says, they leave scratches on the floor and tracks on the carpet and, anyway, they belong in the park.

In Jason's house there is no baby, but one is coming, I think this summer. It's nice and quiet there and *his* mother smiles all the time and they never run out of chocolate pops. Jason's mother lets me use her electric typewriter and she never yells not to break it.

While she's working, she wears skinny gray headphones with private piped-in music. It's neat the way her head bops up and down and sometimes sideways when she types.

The best way to get through a day at my house is to plug your ears at least half the time. I mean, everything comes in *twos* around here—it's twice the screeching and double the banging and slamming and crying. Twins! Who ordered the twins? Did you? I say. My mother calls it ordinary chaos, the sort they have in every house. Not in Jason's, I remind her. Everything is great at Jason's.

Jason has his own room. There's a bunk bed with two ladders but no bunk on the bottom. He sleeps on top, and underneath is a space with a sign that says JASON'S PAD—PRIVATE: DO NOT ENTER UNLESS INVITED. In his room there's a place for everything, and everything is in its place. *His* mother stops by ten times a day to fold his clothes and make his bed and fix his books in perfect rows on the shelf.

My room is big, all right, but it better be, because the you-know-whos have to sleep there too. As babies go they're not so bad, my mother says. They're bad enough, I tell her, bad enough. Just look at this mess, I say. So then she says to get to work—she can't do it all. Well, Jason's mother can! Good for her, my mother says in her quiet-angry voice. Next time, Jessica, you can order up a different mom.

And look at this—I have to wear just bottoms from my baseball
pajamas because the top is in the wash! The thing I want is always in
the wash. It isn't fair, I tell my mother. She understands, she says,
because whatever she wants is always in the wash too. Then she says
to quit complaining, I sound like a grump, and she's had *enough*.

Me too! I've had enough. I call up Jason. He's lucky, I tell him, to have a mom who cooks good old white spaghetti and makes his bed and never yells about motorcycles in the house. You're crazy, he groans. White spaghetti is a drag, and I *hate* neat. It's *dead* around here. I want action!

There's plenty of action here, I say. Maybe your mother wants *me* instead. My mom would sure take you. Maybe we can swap. Jason hangs right up to tell his mother, and I run inside to tell mine. A mommy exchange? My mother nods. Not a bad idea.

We have a meeting. Jason's mother says a mommy exchange is fine with her but just for overnight. My mother thinks a night and a day are better. But Jason and I mean *business*. We're talking for keeps, we explain. Finally we settle on a weekend plan, a Friday to Sunday night exchange. But that is just for starters. And fathers get to visit twice. Fathers *only*.

I pack my purple bag with baseball bottoms and Superman stickers and my favorite book about bears at night. When I ask for a special little case like Jason's to keep my toothbrush clean, my mother says pack it plain, Jessica, just pack it plain. Boy, is she going to be sorry when this mommy exchange gets going.

Jason comes at five. My mother hugs him hello and then she hugs me good-bye and I'm positive Jason's hug was a little bigger than necessary.

Down at Jason's his mother kisses both my cheeks and says how great to have a daughter for the weekend. Don't forget, I say, the weekend's just for starters. Dinner's at seven, she tells me then. Seven? In my house we eat at six, sharp. Well, she says, plugging in her headphones, it's time for work.

I unpack the toothbrush without a case and the baseball bottoms. The pink checkered blanket from my bed looks awful with Jason's sailboat sheets and I bump my head on the ceiling two times in a row. At my house a bump brings my mom with ice-in-a-towel. I think about asking Jason's mother if she knows about ice-in-a-towel, but she's typing hard out there, so I rub my own head this time.

Even though the sign warns DO NOT ENTER UNLESS INVITED, I get to work on my new bear scrapbook down in JASON'S PAD. I trace two koalas, three pandas, and seven grizzly bears. It's so nice and quiet down here, I could probably trace a million. It sure is great not to have those twins scratching and tearing and pulling at my important papers. What pests they are! I bet they miss me. I ought to make them a special picture. I'll drop it off and stay a minute or so. They'll cry like crazy when I say it's time to go back. Sorry, guys, but things are great and super-quiet at Jason's. They really know how to leave a person alone over there.

I take a spin on Jason's motorcycle. I skid and screech and whip around corners. I zoom across shiny wood floors, and his mother doesn't even holler. I think she can't hear me with all that piped-in music that makes her head bop up and down and sometimes sideways. I hold my finger on the siren with batteries. I hold it such a long time it makes a little red mark on my knuckle. Life sure is a breeze at Jason's.

I call Jason, just to make sure he isn't homesick or anything. When my mom answers, I get this funny feeling in my throat. Jessica! I miss you, are you having fun? Of course, I say. Is Jason there?

How's it going? Jason asks. Great, I say. Having fun? Of course, he says, but his voice sounds just a little weird. See you, Jason. So long, Jess.

Seven-fifteen and still no dinner. I put eleven cutouts in an envelope marked FOR THE TWINS, LOVE AND KISSES, JESSICA. When my mom sees that, she'll remember what a thoughtful girl I am and she'll be plenty sorry. At seven-thirty the typing stops. Hurrah! Jason's mother is smiling, as usual. Are we having spaghetti, I ask, very weak, the long stringy white kind? You bet, she says. I try to eat it, really I do, but Jason's mother's spaghetti has this awful way of sticking together, like pasty clumps of dough.

At bedtime Jason's mother says she's tired of bears, and she picks a book about birds at night. It has too many words and not enough pictures and, anyway, who cares about birds at night? She kisses my cheek in a very nice way but doesn't hug and squeeze the way my mother does. And she just forgets, I suppose, to say what a great girl I am and to tell me she loves me to pieces. What about that baby in your stomach? I ask. Next time I have you and Jason in the same room, she says, I'm going to tell you a secret.

In the morning there's hot cereal for breakfast, and I only like it cold. Jason's mother says to quit swishing it around the bowl, which is the kind of thing my mom tells the twins but never me. Then she goes inside to type, and I go back to swishing.

Next time I look up, Jason is standing there in his pajamas. He looks beat. I'll never last the weekend at your house, he sighs. It's crazy up there! The twins jumped all over the bed at five this morning and cried because it wasn't you. Your house is so noisy, he moans, I had to plug my ears half the time. I need quiet! It's just ordinary chaos, I tell him, the sort they have in every house.

Jason's mother gives him some big hug. It reminds me of the way my mom hugs and squeezes, even after a bad day. And now for the secret, she announces, pointing to her stomach. It's twins. She giggles. Twins are coming this summer!

I'm home, I shout, and my mother comes flying from the other room. You're my girl, she says, like it or not. Jason says he won't last the weekend at our house, I explain. He says he needs quiet. Quiet? She laughs. Never heard of it! What about the mommy exchange, I ask. If you want, she says, we can try again sometime. But today, at least, let's stick together. I kind of like it that way.

In Jason's house they get spaghetti at least twice a week. But in my house we get green curls of pasta, and they never, ever stick like pasty clumps of dough.